This book is dedicated to
Eddie, Edna, George, David,
Patrick, Britt, and United
Airlines
Love,
Todd

First published 1999 by
Little, Brown and Company, USA

First published in Great Britain 2001
by Walker Books Ltd
87 Vauxhall Walk, London SE11 5HJ

2 4 6 8 10 9 7 5 3 1

© 1999 Todd Parr

Printed in Hong Kong

British Library Cataloguing in Publication Data:
a catalogue record for this book
is available from the British Library

ISBN 0-7445-8198-2

THINGS THAT MAKE YOU FEEL GOOD

THINGS THAT MAKE YOU FEEL BAD

TODD PARR

WALKER BOOKS
AND SUBSIDIARIES
LONDON • BOSTON • SYDNEY

Bubble baths

Stink BUGS

Good

Hot chocolate with marshmallows

Good

Friends

Bad

Bullies

Good

Tooth Fairy

Bad

Toothache

Good

Sun

The
Dark

Good

kisses

Bad

Mosquito bites

Good

Waves

Bad

Sharks

Good

chicken soup

chicken pox

BiG birthday presents

Bad

BiG Hairy Spiders